Going Fishing

Juliet Partridge

Illustrated by Jackie Morris

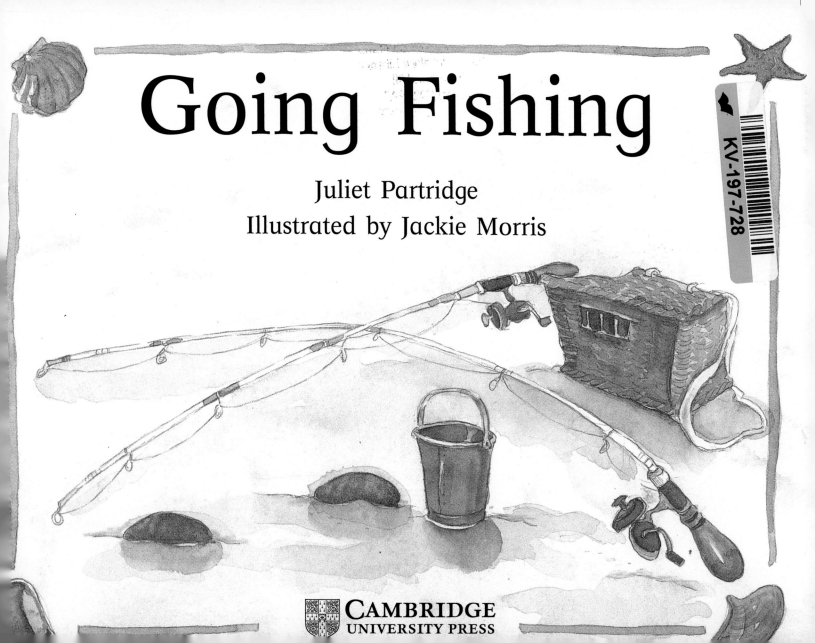

CAMBRIDGE
UNIVERSITY PRESS

When I was six,

we went to the seaside for a holiday.

One day, Dad said, "Let's go fishing."

"Oh good," said Mum.
"Fish for tea tonight."

Dad took his big fishing-rod.

I took my little fishing-rod.

We got a bucket full of worms.

There were hundreds of fish jumping in the water.

There were hundreds of seagulls catching the fish.

We put our fishing lines in the water,
and waited and waited and . . .

. . . waited, but we didn't catch any fish.

"Let's go home," said Dad.
"No fish for tea tonight."

"What will Mum say?" I said.

Just then, a fish fell out of the sky!
We were so surprised.

Seagulls are good at fishing,
I think.